To = Joseph Allan on his 7th B.
March 31 /2008
From - Grandma "Kaye"

D1467465

Robin Hood

Crossing a bridge one day, Robin Hood encountered a big, burly man blocking the way. They fought with their staffs until Robin fell into the river. The giant, whose name was Little John, helped Robin out of the water and then joined his band of Merry Men.

Robin Hood, Little John and Will Scarlet were resting under an oak tree in Sherwood Forest. Little John said he had heard talk of a friar who was almost as good an archer as Robin. "He can shoot a target half a mile away," he said.

Just then, a chubby friar approached the outlaws, across the stream.

"Good day, Friar!" said Robin Hood. "Are you Friar Tuck?"

"Indeed, I am," replied the visitor.

Robin Hood cried out, "Welcome! I hear that you are a wonder with a bow and arrow. Why don't you carry me across the stream and show me how good your aim really is?"

After a moment's hesitation, Friar Tuck agreed. When he was halfway across the stream, the Friar spotted something out of the corner of his eye. He immediately plucked an arrow from his quiver, throwing Robin into the water. His shot hit its target, killing one of the royal deer. Oh no!

Robin Hood hid Friar Tuck in Sherwood Forest where his Merry Men lived. The friar met the rest of the band as well as Robin's companion, the lovely Maid Marian.

The Merry Men stole from the rich to give to the poor and they protected the villagers from the cruel Sheriff of Nottingham.

The next day, the Sheriff left his castle with some knights to escort a chest full of gold and jewels. The Sheriff was sure his treasure was well guarded, but he was sorely mistaken! All of a sudden, dozens of men appeared in the trees. The Merry Men took not only the treasure, but the knights' armor and swords as well!

At a feast at his castle, the Sheriff of Nottingham planned his revenge: he would lure Robin to the castle by holding an archery tournament. Since he was the best archer in the kingdom, Robin would better the Sheriff's archers, giving himself away. And then the Sheriff would have him stopped—at last!

The next day, Little John came upon a notice tacked to a tree. He couldn't read, so he took it to Marian and Robin.

"Why, there is to be an archery tournament. And the prize is a thousand gold coins!" said Marian.

Robin hoped it was not too good to be true.

Robin Hood and his Merry Men prepared
carefully.

On the day of the tournament, the outlaws approached the castle in disguise. Robin Hood rode on a horse in a nobleman's garb, and the others were dressed as peasants and villagers.

The tournament was winding down when the unknown nobleman arrived. Everyone stopped talking as the new challenger stepped forward to the sound of the hunting horn. Whizzz! Robin Hood's arrow sliced the previous leader's arrow right in half!

"Arrest that man!" cried the Sheriff of Nottingham!

His men ran forward but so did the Merry Men, throwing off their disguises and drawing swords and bows. They fought off the Sheriff's men while Robin Hood grabbed the gold and escaped into the woods.

The Merry Men met up with Robin Hood and Maid Marian in a meadow at the edge of Sherwood Forest. The thousand gold coins would go a long way to helping the villagers and peasants. Hurray!